That's What Family's For

Brave
PUBLISHING Co.

That's What Family's For

Book Illustrations © 2023 by Alejandro O'Kif

Published by Brave Books
www.BRAVEbooks.com

ISBN: 978-1-955550-40-6 (paperback)

First English edition published in the USA in 2023

Printed in the United States of America

That's What Family's For

I would, if I could...
⊙ Eat a slice of banana pie the size of a boat.
⊙ Battle a horde of pirates.
⊙ Go to the loudest concert in the world.
⊙ Visit Antarctica.
⊙ Fly to space.

Written by: Dr. Nicole & Hudson Saphier

Art by: Alejandro O'Kif

Jeff loved the summer. He loved swimming, wrestling, and playing basketball with his brothers. But one day while he was running down the court, something didn't feel right.

"I'm sorry, Jeff." Dr. M Paws took Jeff's hand. "You'll need to get plenty of rest. Something is going on with your body that isn't quite right, and unfortunately, it may be this way for a very long time."

Jeff sighed. He wondered why this had to happen to him.

Jeff's mother gave him a tight hug. "This will be hard, my little monkey, but we'll get through it together. That's what family's for."

Jeff knew his mother was right,
but it was hard to be positive.
For the next several days, Jeff
stayed in his room. He watched
the rain fall outside his window,
and he barely touched his soup.

"You know what? Enough of this, let's do something fun!" his mother said. "Let's make a Would-If-I-Could List. If you could do anything you wanted, go anywhere in the world, what would you choose?"

Jeff loved this idea, so he made his list right away.

Jeff knew some of the items on his list were a little silly, but he had fun using his imagination.

I would, if I could...
- Eat a slice of banana pie the size of a boat.
- Battle a horde of pirates.
- Go to the loudest concert in the world.
- Visit Antarctica.
- Fly to space.

The next day, Jeff heard his mother calling, "Jeff! Come here!"

He pulled himself out of bed and opened his door to find ...

Giant strawberries, lakes of chocolate syrup, and roads paved with powdered sugar ... there was a type of food for every color of the rainbow!

He and his mother ran through the candy land together, eating and laughing.

While the pie may not
have been as big as a boat,
it sure was delicious!

The next day, still full from
the dessert extravaganza, Jeff
was walking to his room when
he noticed snow coming from
the hallway.

He peeked around the corner, and the world transformed before him. There were his parents having a snowball fight in a winter wonderland!

Maybe it wasn't a real snowy tundra, but they built an igloo anyway and huddled together with hot chocolate to keep warm.

A few weeks after his winter adventure, when Jeff came home from school, he heard a cry for help. His mom was all tied up, surrounded by a horde of angry pirates.

Jeff jumped up right
away to save his mom.

After Jeff fended off the pirates, his older brother whisked him away to see an awesome monster jam. He soon realized he was the star of the show.

The entire family sang and laughed louder than they had in months. And even though Jeff knew there would be tough days ahead, he realized, with his family by his side, he could face anything.

The next time Dr. M Paws came to visit, he noticed Jeff had a smile on his face. He asked, "What have you been up to, Jeff?"

Jeff responded, "Dr. M Paws, you wouldn't believe me if I told you. I'll have to show you!"

"Wow," breathed Dr. M Paws.
"Family really can make things better."

Jeff grinned. "Very much so."

Hudson Chase was born in 2013 and has always loved the arts. A native of Scottsdale, AZ, Hudson's visual art has been displayed at local museums while his music compositions can be found on various online platforms. Passionate about storytelling, Hudson has been able to use his talent for writing to help communicate and work through his own unexpected life events. With his two brothers, mother and father by his side, Hudson looks to help others dealing with life's ups and downs.

Doctor Nicole Saphier is an internationally recognized physician at Memorial Sloan Kettering Cancer Center, an accomplished media correspondent and host, and the bestselling author of Make America Healthy Again and PANIC ATTACK. Originally from Scottsdale, AZ, Nicole moved to the NYC area and has remained impassioned in her devotion to helping patients and families cope while overcoming many of life's adversities.